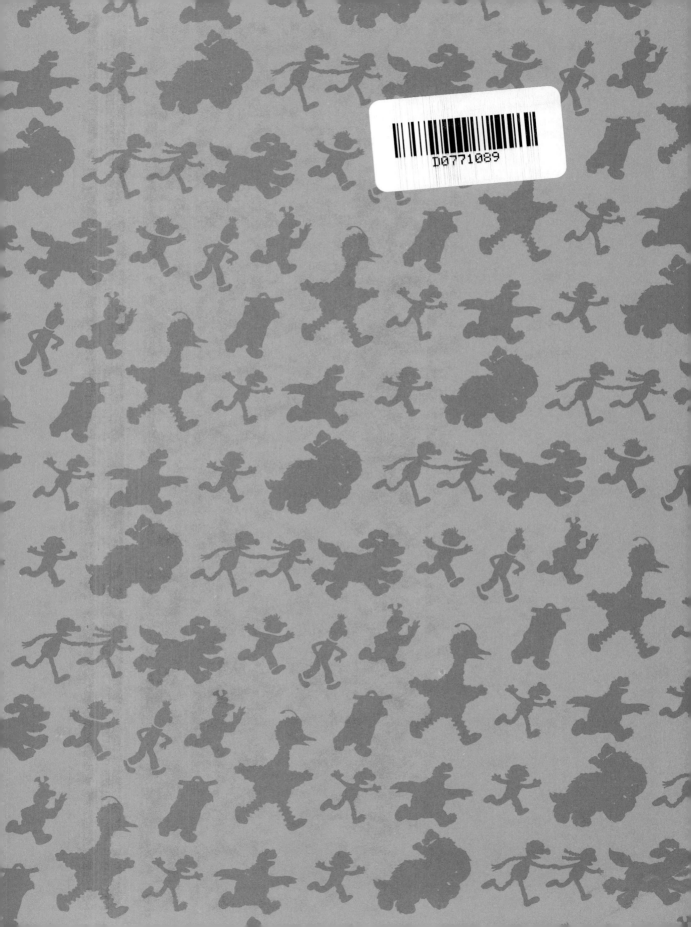

ERNIE'S NEIGHBORHOOD

By Deborah Kovacs
Illustrated by Joe Ewers

On Sesame Street, Susan is performed by Loretta Long,
Gordon by Roscoe Orman, Mr. McIntosh by Chet O'Brien,
and Luis by Emilio Delgado.

A SESAME STREET/GOLDEN PRESS BOOK

Published by Western Publishing Company, Inc.,
in conjunction with Children's Television Workshop.

It was a busy Saturday morning on Sesame Street.
Prairie Dawn was sweeping the sidewalk.
Susan and Gordon were planting in the little garden
in front of 123 Sesame Street.
Big Bird was riding his unicycle.
Ernie was the only one in the neighborhood who
wasn't busy.

"Ernie!" Bert called from the window. "Would you please mail this letter at the post office?"

"Sure, Bert," said Ernie.

"It's my entry in the Bottle Cap Collectors' Contest," said Bert. "The first prize is a trip to the Figgy Fizz Bottling Company. The envelope has to be mailed today, and I promised I'd help Susan and Gordon plant their garden. Can you get there by twelve o'clock? That's when the post office closes."

"You can count on me, old buddy!" said Ernie.

As Ernie passed Oscar's can, Bruno was tossing trash into a big sanitation truck.

"Trash pickup day is my favorite day of the week!" said Oscar. "Look at all this great junk I saved."

"That's nice, Oscar," said Ernie. "But I can't stay. I have to go to the post office to mail this important letter for Bert."

Ernie walked on. As he hurried past the library he heard the librarian reading a story. "Rumpelstiltskin is my name," she read.

"It's Story Hour!" he said to himself. "Mrs. Anderson is reading my favorite story."

Ernie sat down on the library steps and listened to the story until the end.

As he passed by the Playful Pets store, he waved
to the manager. "I don't have time to stop today,"
he called.

But Ernie stopped in the pet store for just a little while.

As Ernie waited at a red light a fire truck zoomed by.
"I wonder where the fire truck is going?" he
thought.
Then he followed it.

The fire truck drove to the fire station and parked inside. Ernie saw the fire fighters climb off the truck. He watched them wash and polish the fire truck.

"Want to help?" asked the captain. He handed Ernie a soft cloth. "You can give that brass bell a good shine!"

Ernie walked on. In the playground outside the
Sesame Street School, kids were playing games.
Grover and some friends were playing softball.

Ernie stopped to watch Herry Monster at bat. Herry
swung and hit the ball. It flew high over the fence.

"I've got it!" cried Ernie, and he ran to catch
the ball.

After the game, Ernie passed Mr. McIntosh's fruit
and vegetable stand. Mr. McIntosh was taking shiny red
apples out of a crate and stacking them.

"Hi, Ernie," said Mr. McIntosh. "Do you want an
apple today?"

"Thanks, Mr. McIntosh," said Ernie. "I'll eat it on
my way to the post office. I have to mail an important
letter for my buddy Bert."

On his way again, Ernie munched his apple. Then he heard a loud whistle shrieking from behind the fence at a construction site. "I'll just peek in for a second," he said.

"The construction site is the busiest place in the neighborhood!" said Ernie as he watched a truck pour cement into buckets. Then he watched a huge crane lift the buckets of cement to the top of the building.

"I'd sure like to run a big crane like that someday," said Ernie.

Ernie meant to hurry past the barbershop, but then
he saw Grover sitting in the barber's chair. Ernie
watched Grover get a fur-cut.

"Just a little bit off the top, please," Grover said to
Mr. Snippit.

As Ernie hurried past Hooper's Store he spotted a sign in the window.

"Monsterberry Crunch is the flavor of the week. My favorite," he said. "Maybe I'll have just one scoop."

Then Ernie heard a strange sound. *Cuckoo! Cuckoo!*
"Where's that bird?" Ernie wondered. He followed
the sound to the Fix-It Shop.
"Luis! What is that noise?" asked Ernie.
"It's Bob's cuckoo clock," said Luis. "I'm fixing it.
Listen."

A bird popped in and out of the clock. "When it sings cuckoo twelve times, that means it's twelve o'clock," said Luis.

"TWELVE O'CLOCK!" cried Ernie. "Oh, no! I have to get Bert's letter to the post office."

Ernie ran out of the Fix-It Shop and down the street.

Ernie's feet pounded up the steps of the post office. He imagined he could hear the cuckoo clock chiming twelve already.

He raced up to a counter. "Please, I have to mail
Bert's Figgy Fizz letter," he said to the postal worker. "I
promised to mail it today. I ran and ran to get here by
twelve." Ernie stopped, out of breath.

"Don't worry," she said. "Your letter will go out
today. You made it just in time."

"Oh, thank you!" said Ernie.

When Ernie got back to Sesame Street, Bert said,
"You missed a busy morning on Sesame Street. Did you
mail my letter in time, Ernie?"
"Sure, Bert," said Ernie. "No problem!"